Welcome Home, Jenny Sutter

Julie Marie Myatt

SAMUEL FRENCH

FOUNDED 1830

SAMUELFRENCH.COM
SAMUELFRENCH-LONDON.CO.UK

FOR PRODUCTION ENQUIRIES

UNITED STATES AND CANADA
Info@SamuelFrench.com
1-866-598-8449

UNITED KINGDOM AND EUROPE
Plays@SamuelFrench-London.co.uk
020-7255-4302

Each title is subject to availability from Samuel French, depending upon country of performance. Please be aware that *WELCOME HOME, JENNY SUTTER* may not be licensed by Samuel French in your territory. Professional and amateur producers should contact the nearest Samuel French office or licensing partner to verify availability.

WELCOME HOME, JENNY SUTTER was first produced by the Oregon Shakespeare Festival (Bill Rauch, Artistic Director) at the New Theatre in Ashland, Oregon on February 24, 2008. The performance was directed by Jessica Thebus, with sets by Richard L. Hay, costumes by Lynn Jeffries, lights by Allen Lee Hughes, and music composition by Paul James Pendergast. The cast was as follows:

JENNY SUTTER	Gwendolyn Mulamba
HUGO	Cameron Knight
LOUISE (LOU)	Kate Mulligan
CHERYL	K.T. Vogt
DONALD	Gregory Linington
BUDDY	David Kelly

CHARACTERS

JENNY SUTTER – thirty, African-American

HUGO – mid-twenties

LOUISE (LOU) – mid-forties

CHERYL – mid to late fifties

DONALD – mid-thirties

BUDDY – mid-forties. Physically handicapped –
body bent awkwardly sideways.

SETTING

Hospital.

Bus station.

Slab City, California

TIME

Present.

Scene One

> *(*JENNY *is alone on a cot, staring at the ceiling. Her upper-body in a bra, her lower body in camouflage uniform. Desert boots beside her. She holds a cell phone, but doesn't use it.)*

JENNY. *(o.s.)* I was born in a one-room apartment over the family Exxon Station in Barstow, California. As a baby, I liked to sit in my father's arms and look out the window. Always facing forward. Both our eyes looking out on the day. "Show me the way, Dad. Guide me. Show me how to live in that world." With my mother, I preferred to sit as close as possible to her chest, heart to heart, not caring what I saw. Not needing to see a thing but her. "Teach me how to love, Mom. Let me feel what love feels like." And when I couldn't sit in either of their arms, because they were too busy floundering apart, I would lay facing the ceiling in my crib. My eyes darting back and forth against the white paint, looking for cracks. "Are you there, God? Is that God up there? Hey, God, if you are up there, can you give me something to believe in? Just come through the cracks and talk to me, OK?" But. The ceiling was quiet. The ceiling never changed. Only the same shadows of my parents dancing across the white, as they stood arguing in a corner of the room… Eventually, I stopped asking. I gave up on the ceiling. I turned my face to the wall instead, where there hung a picture of my dead uncle Jim, killed in Vietnam.

> *(Slide of a 18-year-old man in a U.S. Marine Corps uniform, circa 1969. Smiling for the camera.)*

(o.s.) Slowly I fell asleep in the comfort of his young, beautiful smile…the flickering light of the gold buttons on his proud chest…and I dreamed of being a hero.

> *(The sound of a bomb exploding.)*

> *(Two MPs enter in MP hats. One carries a duffel bag, and sets it down. The men try to carry the cot, with* **JENNY** *on it –)*

Wait.

> *(They finally put the cot down. She slowly stands.)*

I'll make my own way.

> *(The MPs carry the cot off stage, leaving her bag behind.)*

> *(***JENNY*** *reaches in and pulls out civilian clothes. She takes off her boots and uniform, revealing from the knee down, she has a new prosthetic leg.)*

> *(***JENNY*** *carefully puts on jeans and socks and shoes. Then a shirt.)*

> *(She puts her boots and uniform in her bag, and crosses the stage.)*

Scene Two

(The bus station.)

*(She takes out a cigarette and **HUGO** enters.)*

*(**HUGO** plays a lighter; longing for something new to light on fire.)*

HUGO. You can't smoke in here.

*(**JENNY** puts the cigarette away.)*

Where're you going?

JENNY. Where're you going?

HUGO. I work here.

(silence)

You waiting for someone?

JENNY. Are you?

HUGO. I told you, I work here.

JENNY. Then go work.

(silence)

HUGO. This isn't a great place to wait.

(silence)

I'm serious, lady.

JENNY. You gonna burn it down?

*(**HUGO** watches a bug rush by.)*

HUGO. Not yet.
You don't want to be here alone.

JENNY. Who said I was alone?

HUGO. I don't see anyone with you.

JENNY. You the Alone Police?

HUGO. Yeah.

*(**HUGO** sees the bug again.)*

You waiting for someone?

JENNY. I'm waiting for the bus.

HUGO. You missed it.

JENNY. I'll take the next one.

HUGO. It's not for another four hours.

JENNY. Then I guess I'll have to keep waiting.

HUGO. It's a crappy place to wait. This time of night.

JENNY. I've seen worse.

> (**HUGO** *sees the bug across stage again, and rushes over to stomp it…misses it the first time, but gets it the second time.*)

HUGO. Yeah! That's what I'm talking about! Think you can sneak by me?!

> (**HUGO** *inspects his shoe.*)

Now who's the boss, asshole?

> (*He decides to burn the bug off his shoe.*)

Yeah. That's right. Tell your friends.

> (**JENNY** *just looks at him. He finally meets her gaze.*)

Cockroaches freak me out. Running and hiding everywhere. Running and hiding.

> (*He shouts to any bugs who might hear:*)

I'm the fucking boss here!

> (*silence*)

JENNY. Why don't you clean this place? It smells like piss.

HUGO. What's the point. The minute I clean something, some bum just walks in and takes a shit on it.

> (*silence*)

Where are you going?

JENNY. Why don't you work.

HUGO. Seriously. Where you headed?

JENNY. Why?

HUGO. I keep a chart in the office. Who's going where. Why they're going. How long they will be staying. Etc.

JENNY. What for?

HUGO. The hell of it.

JENNY. Really?

HUGO. Have you worked a graveyard shift?

JENNY. Yes.

HUGO. Gotta do something.

JENNY. Trying cleaning.

HUGO. Where you going?

JENNY. Won't you find out when I buy my ticket?

HUGO. Is that your final destination?

JENNY. None of your business.

HUGO. See. That's too unclear. I need a place. A name.

JENNY. I don't want you following me.

HUGO. Why would I follow you?

JENNY. You seem bored.

HUGO. Not that bored.

> *(silence)*

So where are you going?

JENNY. Where's your bathroom?

HUGO. Over there. But I wouldn't use it.

JENNY. Why?

HUGO. Some crackheads just came out of there with their pants down. One of them was carrying all the soap and toilet paper.

> **(JENNY** *takes a deck of cards from her bag.)*

JENNY. The government should hire you.

HUGO. Why?

JENNY. Your work ethic is just what they're looking for.

HUGO. Really?

JENNY. Give them a call.

HUGO. Maybe I will. You know, I've thought about that.

> **(HUGO** *takes out his lighter.)*

I've got no experience, but you know, they could hire me right on the spot or something, you know, just for showing up… I can blow some shit up.

JENNY. You're already qualified.

HUGO. Where are you going? Just tell me.

JENNY. You play Gin?

HUGO. Yeah. Why?

JENNY. I don't want to hear you talk.

      (**JENNY** *deals the cards for a game of Gin.*)

HUGO. You missed at least ten busses. I watched you.

      (*silence*)

I thought, "Maybe she's homeless. Husband threw her out. Maybe she's a prostitute. Moving to Vegas."

JENNY. Why don't you stop worrying about me?

HUGO. I'm not worried about you.

JENNY. Then shut up.

      (**JENNY** *paces.*)

      (**HUGO** *struggles over his cards.*)

Have you played cards before?

HUGO. Of course.

JENNY. Then you know that one of the rules is that you don't make your fellow card player wait for ten fucking minutes while you sit with a shitty hand of cards and try and figure out which shitty card to get rid of.

HUGO. That's not a rule.

JENNY. It is where I come from.

HUGO. Where's that?

JENNY. None of your business.

HUGO. Then the rules don't apply, do they?

      (**JENNY** *waits.*)

      (**HUGO** *inspects his cards, rearranges them in his hand. He almost puts down a card, changes his mind.*)

(*JENNY waits.*)

JENNY. Jesus Christ.

(**HUGO** *carefully rearranges his cards again; almost puts down another card, changes his mind.*)

Just lay down that piece of shit eight of diamonds.

HUGO. How do you know I have the eight of diamonds?

JENNY. Because I don't have it.

HUGO. You looked at my hand?

JENNY. No.

HUGO. Yes you did.

JENNY. No I didn't.

(**LOUISE** *enters with an extremely large suitcase, and a plastic bag full of her personal items.*)

LOU. That bathroom is disgusting. Excuse me, do you work here? Sir?

HUGO. I'm concentrating!

LOU. Do you work here?

(*He finally discards, almost picks it up again, doubting, when –*)

(**JENNY** *picks up the card, and lays out her winning hand.*)

JENNY. Gin! Motherfucker! Gin!

HUGO. You cheated.

JENNY. No I didn't.

LOU. Sir?

HUGO. Yes you did.

LOU. Sir?

JENNY. It was easier to beat you than cheat. Believe me.

HUGO. What's that supposed to mean?

LOU. Sir?

HUGO. What?! Stop calling me sir. I'm not a hundred.

LOU. This station is unacceptable.

HUGO. It's my job to run the bus station and sell tickets. Not police the nasty-ass people who come in here.

LOU. Who lives like that?

HUGO. Will you be buying a ticket today, "ma'am", or just here to complain?

LOU. Yes.

HUGO. Yes, what?

LOU. I'm here to buy a ticket.

HUGO. Where are you going?

LOU. Why?

HUGO. What's the big mystery with you two? You famous?

LOU. Niland.

HUGO. Fine. Booth opens in twenty minutes.

(He exits.)

LOU. Did you see the floor out there? What was that? ...I can't believe I have to wait in this stink hole. I've seen about all I want to see of Los Angeles, I'll tell you that much. Have you been to Hollywood?

JENNY. No.

LOU. Hell with glitter. I'll leave it at that.

JENNY. You play gin?

LOU. Yes. No. Well. I do. I did.

*(**LOU** eyes the cards longingly.)*

I can't play cards anymore.

JENNY. Why?

LOU. I have – had a bit of a gambling problem.

(silence)

Even though I know I'd beat you in a matter of minutes. Seconds maybe. I can't tempt myself. Just thinking of touching the cards makes me...anxious.

(silence)

Of course there are worse things.

(silence)

I had to give up drinking. Cigarettes.

(**LOU** *sighs, continues:*)

Sleeping pills. Aspirin. Diet Coke. Snickers bars. Raisins. Lipstick. Fruit roll-ups.

(*silence*)

(**JENNY** *begins to play a game of solitaire.*)

Where you headed?

JENNY. Where's the next bus going?

LOU. Niland.

JENNY. Where's that?

LOU. Middle of nowhere really. Desert.

JENNY. That's where I'm going.

LOU. Most people think it's a shithole.

(*silence*)

You have family there?

JENNY. No.

LOU. I do. I did. But I had to give them up too.

(*silence*)

Where're you staying?

JENNY. I haven't been thinking that far ahead.

LOU. There's not a lot out there.

JENNY. I'll be fine.

LOU. Nothing.

(**LOU** *inspects* **JENNY**'*s solitaire game.*)

You can move that eight…on the nine.

(*They look at the game together.* **JENNY** *moves the card.*)

I have a place. If you need it. I can make room. I mean, it's not much. Don't expect a palace.

JENNY. I'm not used to much.

LOU. Me either.

> *(**LOU** and **JENNY** share an awkward smile.)*

You think that says something about us?

JENNY. What?

LOU. That we don't expect much… My shrink Cheryl tells me I have self-esteem issues. Among my other more obvious issues. Wow. My life. What a burden.

> *(**LOU** sighs.)*

I'm a rock in a hard place. But. I guess I'm kinda settling into it.

> *(**LOU** smiles, pleasantly. Points to **JENNY**'s shirt.)*

That color's nice on you. Where are you from?

JENNY. Barstow.

LOU. Now *that* is a shithole town.

JENNY. Yeah, well, I left it. A long time ago.

LOU. What'd you leave it for? A man?

JENNY. A job.

LOU. What do you do?

> *(silence)*

JENNY. I just retired.

LOU. Retired? How old are you?

JENNY. Thirty.

LOU. Thirty? What the hell did you retire from? Gymnastics?

JENNY. The Marine Corps.

LOU. Wow. A Marine? You?

JENNY. Yep.

LOU. I'm trying to picture it… Uniform?

JENNY. Uh huh.

LOU. Boots?

JENNY. Uh huh.

LOU. Gun?

JENNY. Mmm hmm.

LOU. Iraq?

JENNY. Yeah.

LOU. Really? When'd you get home?

JENNY. Last night.

LOU. Last night?

(*silence*)

Well, hell. What are you doing here? Where's your family? Where's the band? Where's the parade?

JENNY. You're looking at it.

LOU. Shit.

(**LOU** *hugs her.*)

Is this turning you on?

JENNY. No. Not really.

LOU. Lesbian?

JENNY. No.

LOU. Are you sure?

JENNY. Positive.

LOU. I heard all women in the military were lesbians.

JENNY. No. But there's opportunity. If you're into that.

LOU. What about the men?

JENNY. What about them?

LOU. There are a lot of men… Obviously.

JENNY. Yes.

LOU. Away from home… I hear those ladies over there don't have sex.

JENNY. It's a different culture. That way –

LOU. I mean, how could they with all those clothes. All that fabric. A guy would need a map and a flashlight to find it.

(**LOU** *smiles at herself.*)

Did they come after you?

(**JENNY** *pulls away from* **LOU.**)

Wish I didn't have to give that up.

JENNY. You had to give up sex?

LOU. I'm an addict. Anything fun or pleasurable, I can't stop myself.

JENNY. Well, these men are not all that pleasurable.

LOU. Still. I miss it. I miss it a lot.

> *(silence)*

But, you know, as long as I keep myself in motion, I'm OK. I forget about it. Just keep in motion, taking buses here and there. Move every month. Don't think about it. Go home for awhile when I get tired, then head out again…go go go.

> *(She sighs.)*

Only now I think I'm addicted to moving… Kind of a quandary, huh?

> *(**HUGO** enters.)*

HUGO. You going to Niland or not?

LOU. Why?

HUGO. You haven't bought your ticket.

LOU. What's your hurry?

HUGO. The bus is coming.

> *(**JENNY** picks up her stuff.)*

And I already wrote you on my goddamn chart. I don't want to erase it.

LOU. Try erasing this smell. Could take years.

> *(He exits.)*

> *(**LOU** tries to sum **JENNY** up.)*

Let me ask you something. Why would you want to go out to the desert?

JENNY. Why not?

LOU. You just got back from a desert.

JENNY. So.

LOU. Don't you want to go home?

JENNY. What's it matter to you –

LOU. Well, don't you want to go someplace nice? Treat yourself nice. Someplace cool and relaxing. Maybe a spa or something.

> (*silence*)

Do you have a family to go home to?

> (**JENNY** *begins to exit.*)

JENNY. I don't want to miss the bus.

> (**JENNY** *exits and* **LOU** *hurriedly picks up the cards and puts them in her pocket. Drags her suitcase offstage.*)

Scene Three

BUDDY. *(offstage, singing hymn, "Softly and Tenderly")*
SOFTLY AND TENDERLY, JESUS IS CALLING
CALLING FOR YOU AND FOR ME
SEE, ON THE PORTALS HE'S WAITING AND WATCHING
WATCHING FOR YOU AND FOR ME…

> *(**LOU** struggles to carry both of their luggage on stage.)*

LOU. Welcome to Slab City.

> *(**LOU** wasn't kidding. It's not much. It's an empty spot of concrete.)*

JENNY. I thought we were going to Niland –

> *(**JENNY** takes her bag from **LOU**.)*

LOU. I talked the bus driver into a taking us the extra miles.

> *(**LOU** walks **JENNY** across the stage, waving to folks left and right, as **BUDDY** continues to sing offstage, she keeps talking.)*

BUDDY. *(offstage, singing)*
COME HOME, COME HOME
YE WHO ARE WEARY, COME HOME
EARNESTLY, TENDERLY, JESUS IS CALLING
CALLING, O CHILDREN, COME HOME…

LOU. Hi Page! …Hi Ricky! …How ya doing, Marcus! Your plants look great. That toilet makes a terrific planter… Donald.

> *(**DONALD** passes across stage and exits.)*

DONALD. Louise.

LOU. Hi Linda! …Nice chairs. Wow. Where'd you find those? …Ola, Raul. Love your shorts.

JENNY. You have a lot of friends.

LOU. Luckily I didn't have to give them up. Yet. Oh gosh, and here comes Buddy. And I look like shit. If it weren't for that disgusting bus station…

(BUDDY enters, whistling the rest of the hymn, carrying some of LOU's things: A camping lamp. A family portrait of a family of seven. Bedding. A tarp. He sets the stuff up around the women.)

BUDDY. Hi Louise.

LOU. Hi Buddy.

BUDDY. You look nice.

LOU. Oh please… I do not. Thanks for watching my place.

BUDDY. No problem. No problem at all.

LOU. You look good.

BUDDY. I got a haircut. Who's this?

LOU. This is Jenny.

BUDDY. Jenny who?

LOU. Jenny…

JENNY. Sutter.

BUDDY. Jenny Sutter. Sounds like a housewife's name. Are you a housewife?

JENNY. No –

LOU. She's a Marine.

BUDDY. A Marine.

LOU. And she's not a lesbian. I already asked her.

BUDDY. My grandfather was a Marine. World War II.

JENNY. Really?

BUDDY. I used to have his medals. You get any medals?

JENNY. No.

BUDDY. Well, I had them until I gave them to some kid last year. I wasn't using them, and the kid wanted them so bad, I said, what the hell. I'm not sentimental. He wore them on his t-shirt.

LOU. Buddy's a preacher.

BUDDY. Unofficially.

LOU. Got his license on the internet.

BUDDY. It came with a free credit check.

LOU. He holds services.

BUDDY. To those who want to listen.

LOU. And feeds the hungry.

BUDDY. When I can.

LOU. We had an affair.

BUDDY. Before she gave up sex.

LOU. It was wild.

BUDDY. Sort of.

LOU. I'd marry him, but.

BUDDY. I'm off limits.

LOU. He's already married.

BUDDY. I just can't find my wife.

LOU. She ran off with one of his friends.

BUDDY. What can you do.

LOU. He's never bitter.

BUDDY. I'm not?

LOU. I love him.

BUDDY. Please.

LOU. I do.

BUDDY. You're embarrassing me.

LOU. Am I?

BUDDY. Yes.

LOU. Why?

BUDDY. You know how I feel about you.

LOU. It's the same way I feel about you.

BUDDY. So let's not talk about it.

LOU. I really do like your haircut. That last style you had
was just too New Wave for you –

BUDDY. I'm not the New Wave sort.

LOU. I know –

BUDDY. I don't even know what New Wave is.

LOU. Well, it began in the '80s –

JENNY. I need to lay down.

LOU. She's been to war.

BUDDY. No kidding.

LOU. No kidding.

BUDDY. I mean I guess I shouldn't be surprised.

LOU. We are at war.

BUDDY. She'll need a good rest from that one.

LOU. What a mess.

BUDDY. Whew.

LOU. Take my bed.

BUDDY. Good idea. Don't make her sleep on the couch.

LOU. There is no couch.

BUDDY. Where are you going to sleep?

LOU. Beside her.

BUDDY. I don't know. I don't know if your shrink Cheryl will like that –

LOU. I'll tell her we're camping.

BUDDY. Why?

LOU. Camping changes the rules on everything.

BUDDY. It does?

LOU. Yeah.

BUDDY. How?

LOU. Camping is just surviving in the wild. And survival changes the rules, Buddy. Everybody knows that.

BUDDY. Oh.

LOU. *(to* **BUDDY***)* Help me make the bed.

JENNY. I'll help –

LOU. You're my guest. Relax.

> *(They make up a bed together.* **JENNY** *watches, getting sleepier. She sits down.)*

BUDDY. I hear my grandfather slept for one month solid when he came home from war.

LOU. Wow.

BUDDY. He'd just wake up every eight hours and eat a sandwich and drink a beer, then go back to sleep. Incredible. Never spoke a word about it. When the month was over, he simply went to work on the farm. End of story. Except for his medals, of course. I guess those spoke for themselves. He was brave, my grandpa. Brave and mean.

LOU. Don't tuck the sheets in so tight.

BUDDY. That's how it's done.

LOU. Where?

BUDDY. In the military.

LOU. Not here.

BUDDY. You know I slept here a few times.

LOU. Why?

BUDDY. I don't know. Old time's sake.

LOU. How was it?

BUDDY. Lonely.

LOU. What were you expecting?

BUDDY. Comfort, I guess.

LOU. You're just an old romantic, Buddy.

BUDDY. Or a fool.

LOU. There we go.

>*(The bed is finished. **JENNY** has fallen asleep on the floor.)*

BUDDY. Should we move her?

LOU. No. Let her sleep.

BUDDY. Let's at least take off her shoes.

>*(They remove **JENNY**'s shoes.)*

>*(Both are silent for a moment as they look at **JENNY**'s leg.)*

LOU. Everyone should have someone to take off their shoes.

>*(**LOU** watches as **BUDDY** puts the blanket over **JENNY**, and carefully places her shoes beside her.)*

Let me come over to your place for awhile, Buddy. I want to watch some television.

BUDDY. We can do that.

LOU. You can't touch me, of course.

BUDDY. Of course.

>　(**LOU** *turns out the light.*)

LOU. But I have missed you.

BUDDY. That goes without saying.

>　(*They exit.*)

LOU. *(offstage)* I think I traveled too far this time.

BUDDY. *(offstage)* Where'd you go?

LOU. *(offstage)* Oh. Too far. Just too far.

BUDDY. *(offstage)* Do you need me to take off your shoes?

LOU. *(offstage)* I need you to take off my feet.

>　(**JENNY** *turns on the light. Sees her shoes beside her.*)
>
>　(*She picks up one of her shoes, and puts it back on the prosthetic foot.*)
>
>　(*She turns off the light.*)

Scene Four

(Morning.)

*(**LOU** lays beside **JENNY** in the bed. Both women have their eyes closed, not ready to open them on the new day.)*

LOU. You scream and talk in your sleep, you know.

JENNY. I do?

LOU. It's pretty awful.

JENNY. Sorry.

LOU. No problem.

(silence)

I just wonder what they feel like?

JENNY. What?

LOU. Your nightmares.

JENNY. I don't know.

LOU. What do you mean, you don't know?

JENNY. I don't remember them.

*(**LOU** opens her eyes.)*

LOU. Really?

JENNY. Yes.

LOU. Nothing?

(silence)

Seriously?

*(**JENNY** opens her eyes.)*

JENNY. Did I hurt you – I didn't hurt you did I?

LOU. No. But it sounded like you took some punches.

JENNY. I didn't hurt you though?

LOU. No.

JENNY. Good.

LOU. I probably would have tried to punch you back… But I gave up fighting.

(silence)

Did those men ever hit you?

JENNY. What men?

LOU. Soldiers.

(silence)

JENNY. Some. If they needed to.

(silence)

LOU. What'd you do over there? In Iraq.

(silence)

You don't have to talk about it…

JENNY. I worked at a checkpoint.

LOU. Checkpoint?

JENNY. For cars and trucks.

LOU. Doing what?

JENNY. Searching people. Women, mostly.

LOU. For what?

JENNY. Explosive devices.

LOU. What are those?

JENNY. Bombs.

(silence)

LOU. You find anything?

(silence)

I wasn't going to ask about all that…or say anything about the…but, since we're sharing the same bed, I guess I thought it wouldn't hurt…to ask.

(silence)

I wouldn't want to pry, but I did want to offer some help if you need it.

(silence)

Shoot. I've got so much shit. I've got so many scars, I've lost count. My back is just… And for awhile, I thought, you know, what the hell. It's only skin. It will heal. No one will see it. I like t-shirts. They're fun. And then one day… I left my husband when I got out of the hospital and walked all the way here. That's when I met Buddy. And my shrink Cheryl. Though I think it's Buddy that's taught me the most. He's really something.

JENNY. What's his deal?

LOU. What do you mean?

JENNY. Does he have, have M.S. or –

LOU. Talk about beating.

> *(sighs)*

That Buddy was beat to a pulp as a kid. I mean, from what I've been able to get out of him, he was his parents' punching bag. Even as a baby. He's all twisted up like that from their beatings. Years of broken bones and healing wrong.

JENNY. Jesus.

LOU. Until finally, some lady saw him with his mother in a grocery store, and stole him out of the shopping cart. Literally, just took him right out of the shopping cart where he was sitting, waiting for his mother to find something down another aisle, and took him straight home with her. Now this lady, Mabel, and her husband had six kids already, and were strapped to take in another, but she could see what was going on. They raised him after that. Just like one of their own. Buddy's real parents never came looking for him. Not once. He had those damn war medals from his grandpa in his pocket. That's all he had of his family. I think he was six or seven then.

JENNY. Jesus. Where's my shoelace?

LOU. Wait, no, he was nine. He's preaching today. I told him we'd come listen.

JENNY. No.

LOU. Why?

JENNY. I'm not a religious person.

LOU. You were praying in your dreams.

> *(silence)*

And you were having several arguments. Including a pretty heated one with God.

JENNY. That's impossible.

LOU. I heard you.

JENNY. I don't believe in God.

> *(silence)*

LOU. You want me to tell you what you said?

JENNY. No.

LOU. Why not?

JENNY. I've got enough on my mind.

LOU. You said –

JENNY. I mean it. I've got enough.

LOU. Your family?

> **(JENNY** *stands up, puts on her shoes. One of her shoelaces is missing.)*

I told Buddy you'd come listen to him speak.

JENNY. I don't believe in that shit. I don't even know what the hell I'm doing here. What is this place? Where's my fucking shoe lace?

> **(LOU** *stands up.)*

LOU. I haven't seen it.

JENNY. Goddamn it –

LOU. Let's make some coffee. I'm starving. You kept me up with your yelling and carrying on and singing... You've got a pretty good voice... At one point I had to join in. We did a pretty good duet...You started singing that Barbara Streisand/Neil Diamond song, "You don't bring me flowers."

JENNY. Bullshit –

LOU. I can't resist a duet.

JENNY. What the hell happened to my shoelace?

(**BUDDY** *enters. Smiles at* **LOUISE** *and* **JENNY**. *Mouths: "Morning."*)

(*He begins to set up a small pulpit.*)

Scene Five

BUDDY. I, I uh –

> (**BUDDY** *clears his throat for his sermon, and addresses the audience.*)

I want to thank ya'll for coming out today. I see a few new faces in the crowd, and that always makes my morning. Not because I think I'm something special or anything, or that ya'll have come to hear me say something important, because I probably won't say something all that important, I mean, unless it strikes you as such, and that would be great, but, you know, I like to keep expectations low…keep the expectations low, but the spirits high…that's kind of my philosophy… keep your life above any kind of expectations and you just might not be disappointed… (I'm already rambling)… Whew… OK… The reason I like to see new faces out here is that I think, hey, look there, some folks are gonna meet some new people, maybe find a new friend, maybe find something in common, maybe share a story out here at Slab City. That's a pretty good start to a day, I think. A new friend. A common interest. A story you haven't heard before. I mean, you really can go to bed after that. Your day is complete. Good night, Irene. Or Jim. Or Mabel. Whatever your name may be. Sleep tight, with your new experience under your pillow. Maybe the tooth fairy will come leave you a quarter for it. Before it slips away… Which makes me think about someone.

> (**BUDDY** *takes a sip of water from a bottle.*)

That's good water.

> (**BUDDY** *reads the label on the bottle.*)

"From the majestic mineral springs of central Arkansas." Central Arkansas. Huh. I've been there. Didn't know they had mineral springs there… Must be hidden… Where was I… Oh, right. I was thinking of a man named Larry Larson. Larry Larson and his wife, Susan, drove their RV out here once. Stayed about a month or two. They were from some place in…let's see…

LOU. *(shouts out)* Ohio.

BUDDY. Ohio. Thank you… Now, as I quickly learned, Larry didn't care much for his oldest daughter's personality. He'd tell you that, straight out, first thing, "I have four daughters. Three of them I get. One of them is a complete mystery. A foreigner. I don't know what planet she came from, but I think it's full of hippies, communists, and nincompoops." That was how he'd speak of his oldest daughter, Janet. Now I never met Janet, but I suppose if I were her, that kind of thing might hurt my feelings. But Larry Larson didn't care. He never had one thing good to say about her: "She's crazy. She's needy. She hugs too much. She talks my f-ing ear off. She's pregnant with the baby of some man who makes dog sweaters for a living. She's given up all food items that begin with A and C. She's gonna have her baby on a cedar bed surrounded by the SPCA." Etc. Well. One day, while Larry Larson was here, he and Susan got a call from their daughter's husband. There had been complications during the delivery of their grandson, and Janet didn't make it. Janet died. Well, word got around, and so we all started bringing flowers to their RV. We knew they'd be heading home the next day, but we all wanted to show our respects, as best we could. Everyone liked Larry and Susan. He played a mean game of horseshoes, and she was an excellent cook. Made many meals for the hungry folks out here. As I was laying my flowers in front of his door, Larry came outside to talk to me. I stuck out my hand to shake his, and I said, "I'm so sorry, Larry. I know this is a terrible loss. I know you loved Janet". He took my hand, and he held it for a long time, and then he finally said, "I loved her more than the others. I actually loved her the best, Buddy. I just don't – didn't know how to love her as my daughter, you see. I didn't know how to love her as someone I couldn't understand. She made me uncomfortable. She embarrassed me. I thought she made me look bad. Because she was never just a person coming into a room, she was an experience. She brought change with her. She brought laughs and chaos. She was never predictable.

Something always happened when she was around. Something interesting… I sure hope my grandson is like her. I do. And not that damn son-in-law. He's so ordinary. I'll never know what she saw in him." Then he let go of my hand, and looked over at all the flowers in front of his RV, and I could tell he was getting ready to cry. He opened the door to go back inside. Before he closed the door he asked me to please thank everyone for the flowers and to please not let them go to waste. "Make sure those flowers get in some water, Buddy," he said. "Make sure everyone gets to enjoy them after we're gone. They paid good money for those."

(**BUDDY** *takes another sip of his water.*)

I can't believe this water is from Arkansas. Unbelievable. I missed it. Huh… Anyway, I guess I've taken about enough of your time this morning. I've put out some coffee and it looks like someone made a delicious looking bundt cake. Thank you to whoever brought that. That took some time and generosity. And thank you to those who came out to hear me speak. I never know what I'm gonna say up here. Except welcome to the new folks. I generally wing it from there. I guess I was thinking of Larry Larson this morning because I remembered the postcard he sent me last week. His grandson just turned five. And apparently, the boy talks constantly, hugs everyone he meets, and has given up all food items that begin with B and D.

(**BUDDY** *raises the water bottle in a toast:*)

Amen, Larry.

Scene Six

CHERYL. Amen.

>(**CHERYL** *and* **DONALD** *have joined* **JENNY** *and* **LOU.**)

LOU. Jenny, I'd like you to meet my shrink, Cheryl.

CHERYL. Jenny.

LOU. Jenny's just back from Iraq.

CHERYL. Wonderful.

LOU. Yeah.

CHERYL. Wonderful.

LOU. Yeah.

CHERYL. Wonderful.

JENNY. Yeah.

>(*silence*)

LOU. If you will excuse me, I'm going to go thank Buddy – I thought that was just lovely –

CHERYL. Where you been Lou?

LOU. Around.

DONALD. I thought that was just bullshit.

LOU. *(to* **JENNY***)* This is Donald. Donald sells jewelry –

DONALD. I don't just sell –

CHERYL. You look terrible. You need a session. I can tell.

>(**CHERYL** *leads* **LOU** *off stage.*)

DONALD. She needs you to tell her what to do next.

LOU. No. I don't.

CHERYL. Back off, Donald.

DONALD. You back off.

>(*They exit.* **JENNY** *is left alone with* **DONALD.**)

>(*silence*)

Iraq, huh?

JENNY. Yep.

DONALD. What are you doing out here?

JENNY. Do you have any booze?

DONALD. Like what?

JENNY. Anything.

DONALD. I keep some tequila in my truck.

JENNY. Feel like sharing it?

DONALD. Uh. I guess. Sure. Uh, wait. I guess wait here.

(**DONALD** *exits, leaving* **JENNY** *alone.*)

(**JENNY** *looks at her hands. Stands awkwardly on stage by herself. Looks at her cell phone. Doesn't use it. Stands waiting. She's looks for cigarettes in her pocket, but she's out. Finds the bullet. Puts it back.*)

(**DONALD** *returns.*)

JENNY. That was fast.

DONALD. I used to run track.

JENNY. Me too.

DONALD. Were you good?

JENNY. Some days.

DONALD. I won a lot of races. It's pretty mental. Running.

(*silence*)

It's just a big mind game. Legs and heart and talent, they really have nothing to do with it.

(*silence*)

DONALD. Just a mind game. To win. I was good at it.

(**DONALD** *offers her the tequila. She takes a swig.*)

JENNY. What's the deal with this place?

DONALD. What do you mean?

JENNY. Seems like it's just a bunch of freaks and old people out here.

DONALD. It's kinda off the map.

JENNY. Why's it called Slab City?

DONALD. It's an old military base.

JENNY. You're kidding?

DONALD. Marine, I think.

(*She hands him back the bottle. Looks around.*)

JENNY. No shit.

DONALD. Now it's just concrete. Full of people figuring their shit out.

JENNY. Do they?

DONALD. What?

JENNY. Figure it out?

DONALD. Who knows.

JENNY. What's your deal?

DONALD. I don't know you well enough.

JENNY. Did you figure it out?

DONALD. I don't know you well enough.

(*silence*)

JENNY. You're kind of handsome, you know that.

(*silence*)

DONALD. Most people wouldn't call me handsome.

JENNY. What would they call you?

(*He shrugs.*)

DONALD. Donald.

(*silence*)

I'm not very social. I generally keep to myself.

(*silence*)

I'm better when I keep to myself.

(*silence*)

I guess some call me indifferent.

JENNY. Are you?

DONALD. Probably. About most things.

JENNY. Why?

DONALD. Seems easier.

JENNY. You want to kiss me?

> (*silence*)

DONALD. Now?

JENNY. Why not?

> (*silence*)

DONALD. It's broad daylight.

JENNY. Is that a problem?

DONALD. Yes.

JENNY. Is there something wrong with me?

DONALD. Not that I know of.

JENNY. You more of a sundown kind of person?

DONALD. Maybe.

> (*silence*)

JENNY. Well, you have plans at sundown?

DONALD. Not that I know of.

JENNY. I guess I have a kiss to look forward to.

> (*silence*)

DONALD. Did you kill anyone over there?

> (*silence*)

Did you?

JENNY. What?

DONALD. Kill anyone.

JENNY. That's a stupid question.

DONALD. I was just curious.

> (*silence*)

DONALD. Always wondered what it felt like. To kill someone, in battle. I've heard some guys admit that they found it exhilarating. Man…that makes you wonder about people. What war does to them. Where their minds go.

> (*silence*)

But this one…everybody knows…this is a bullshit war, don't you think?

JENNY. (Fuck you.)

>	(*silence*)

DONALD. I guess there won't be any kissing.

>	(**JENNY** *takes several big drinks from the bottle.*)

>	(**DONALD** *takes the bottle away from her, checks to see if there's any left, and exits.*)

>	(**JENNY** *touches her lips.*)

>	(*She looks at her leg.*)

Scene Seven

(**CHERYL** *is taking notes as she follows* **LOU** *onstage.*)

LOU. I can't help it. I want something every second. I want a drink. I want a drug. I want to reach out and grab someone. I want to take my clothes off. Have a good time. Be out of control. I want to roll the dice. Take a chance. Hit the big time…I want. I want. I want.

CHERYL. But you don't. You resist. You're strong.

(silence)

LOU. Last night all I wanted to do was do something wild, feel something new. A crack in my brain. Instead I drank a glass of water and swallowed a multi-vitamin. What kind of life is that?

CHERYL. Calm. Steady.

LOU. Miserable. Stupid.

CHERYL. You wanted to feel in control of your life.

LOU. I know.

CHERYL. You didn't want to be a victim to your addictions anymore. Your "wants".

LOU. Now I'm a victim of what I can't have.

CHERYL. Which is better?

LOU. Guess.

CHERYL. It takes time. Let time be your friend. Make friends with time.

LOU. I have enough friends.

(silence)

Maybe my wants are who I am.

CHERYL. No –

LOU. And everything that I constantly desire, is me.

CHERYL. No –

LOU. Denying myself those things, is denying my true self. I'm just a full-fledged wanter. Why can't I be that?

CHERYL. You just can't.

LOU. Why not?

CHERYL. Because That makes you unhappy.

LOU. So does this. I don't know who I am anymore. But a person who spends her day saying, "no" … "don't" … "you can't" … "stop" … "eat a carrot instead".

CHERYL. I love carrots.

LOU. I don't.

CHERYL. You drunk and stoned in bed with someone you don't know, or waking up locked in a trash can, or walking naked across the Golden Gate Bridge –

LOU. It was the Bay Bridge. And I was wearing socks, thank you –

CHERYL. Isn't more true to who you are, than the mild-mannered person who sits quietly having a nice cup of coffee and a decent conversation.

LOU. At a certain point, opinions and coffee breath are not that interesting… I see other people enjoying things and I hate them for it.

(**JENNY** *walks between them.*)

JENNY. Do you have any booze?

CHERYL. No. I do not.

JENNY. Drugs?

CHERYL. Most certainly not.

JENNY. Cigarettes?

CHERYL. Cancer sticks? No, ma'am.

LOU. You want a vitamin?

(**JENNY** *keeps walking.*)

She could use your help.

CHERYL. Obviously.

LOU. She won't ask for it.

CHERYL. I'll find a way.

LOU. She's really –

CHERYL. I thought we were here to talk about you.

LOU. I mean. Look. She's confused. Messed up.

CHERYL. We're talking about you.

LOU. We are talking about me.

CHERYL. What's Jenny have to do with you?

LOU. I want to help her.

CHERYL. You want to help her or you want to be her? Just because she's looking for a party. You want to sell your soul for a good time?

LOU. I want. Period.

CHERYL. But you resist. You resist temptation.

LOU. Uh huh.

CHERYL. Feels good, doesn't it?

LOU. No. I'm bored.

CHERYL. Now we're getting somewhere.

LOU. We are?

CHERYL. That's inner peace, Lou.

LOU. It is?

CHERYL. Absolutely. And I'm proud of you.

  (**CHERYL** *exits.* **LOU** *follows.*)

LOU. Really?

Scene Eight

BUDDY. How you doing down there?

   (**JENNY** *lays on the ground.*)

   (**BUDDY** *hovers over her.*)

 It's cold out here. Are you cold?

JENNY. No.

BUDDY. You sure?

JENNY. Yes.

BUDDY. Lou was looking for you.

JENNY. Why?

BUDDY. She's worried about you.

JENNY. Why?

BUDDY. She wants you to talk to her shrink, Cheryl.

JENNY. (Fuck off.)

   (*silence*)

BUDDY. OK.

   (**BUDDY** *hums a hymn.*)

 Are you missing anything from your stuff?

JENNY. Like what?

BUDDY. Personal items?

JENNY. I don't know.

BUDDY. You drunk?

JENNY. Sort of.

BUDDY. By yourself?

JENNY. A few people helped out. A cup here. A glass there. But I ran the first guy off. Before I could get a kiss out of him.

BUDDY. Who?

JENNY. I think his name was Donald.

BUDDY. You don't want to kiss him.

JENNY. Why not?

BUDDY. He's indifferent.

JENNY. So am I.

BUDDY. You want to talk about it?

JENNY. No.

BUDDY. I'm not a shrink, but I'm a preacher.

JENNY. I heard.

BUDDY. I'm a pretty good listener.

JENNY. Uh huh.

BUDDY. Did you like my sermon?

> (**JENNY** *shrugs.*)

Though I really hate to call it a sermon... I think that's a little fancy for what I do. I kinda just ramble on.

JENNY. Yes. Bullshit.

> (*silence*)

BUDDY. If you don't mind me saying. You seem a little out of sorts. With your life.

JENNY. You want to kiss me?

BUDDY. I'm sorry?

JENNY. Would you like to kiss me?

> (*silence*)

BUDDY. I hadn't really thought about that.

> (*silence*)

JENNY. Why not?

BUDDY. Outside my wife, I'm kinda save myself for Lou.

JENNY. She gave up kissing.

BUDDY. I know.

JENNY. That's dumb.

BUDDY. Still. I think she'd feel betrayed.

JENNY. If you say so.

BUDDY. It hurts to be betrayed like that.

JENNY. If you say so.

BUDDY. Feels more lonely than anything.

> (*silence*)

Although, lonely comes in a lot different colors –

JENNY. Please –

BUDDY. I think that one was red. Bright red. When my mother died, everything was green for about a year or so. Kind of khaki. Then I got a shade of blue that lasted about four years. Never could figure out what started it. I just couldn't shake it. I might still have some of it.

>   *(silence)*

A little bit of blue. Hanging on to my fingers.

>   *(silence)*

Well. I'm here if you need to talk to someone. I'm a better talker than I am kisser anyway. That's what my wife thought.

>   *(silence)*

I never could seem to love her enough. Or Lou.

>   *(silence)*

JENNY. Do you think I'm ugly?

BUDDY. No.

>   *(He takes off his coat and puts it on her.)*

Not at all, Jenny.

>   *(**BUDDY** exits, singing hymn, "I am a Pilgrim.")*

(offstage) I am a pilgrim and a stranger
TRAVELING THROUGH THIS WEARISOME LAND
AND I'VE GOT A HOME IN THAT YONDER CITY, GOOD LORD
AND IT'S NOT (GOOD LORDY IT'S NOT) NOT MADE BY
>   HAND…

>   *(**JENNY** sits up and cries.)*

Scene Nine

(**BUDDY** *stands before his pulpit.*)

BUDDY. OK. It's come to my attention, that there is something not being said here… I recognize that this is called a "pulpit" and many have abused that term – myself included, I imagine – gone on and on about things that no one really wants to listen to. But –

(**JENNY** *walks right in front of him, hands him his jacket.*)

Hi Jenny.

JENNY. Hi.

BUDDY. Where you going?

JENNY. To sleep.

(*She keeps walking.*)

BUDDY. But. But. Expressed. Some things just have to be said no matter what. Put out in the open…

(**BUDDY** *takes a breath.*)

Someone is stealing things in the Slabs. This is a small community. This is a trusting community. I might go as far to say, it is a community built on trust… Being that many of us are strangers coming together here… Trust is the foundation we sit on, just underneath the concrete, trust holds us together. Like any society, it is trust that keeps us civil. When that trust is broken, we all sit on fear and doubt. A kind of erosion slinks through the air. A breakdown of the fabric of society… This stealing someone is causing a breakdown of our society…and what is this person stealing?… What is the culprit denying our citizens, in the privacy of their own homes? Toiletries. Personal items. Lipstick. Blush. Perfume.

LOU. Q-tips. Shampoo.

BUDDY. Q-tips. Shampoo. Curlers. A treasured comb. Tweezers passed down from a beloved grandmother. Eye shadow.

CHERYL. Ointment.

BUDDY. That, yes. Eye lash curler. Wrinkle cream. Teeth whiteners.

> (**BUDDY** *smooths back his hair, missing his prized hair gel.*)

Hair gel.

> (**BUDDY** *scans the audience.*)

Imagine the invasion one feels at having these things stolen from the most private areas of one's home. The medicine cabinet. The Dopp kit. The bathroom closet. Places that are known as the quiet secret keepers, the hidden spaces of vanity. Rummaged through, for what? A half a tube of denture cream? A forgotten bottle of Grecian hair dye? Why? Only the thief knows, I guess. The rest of us are just victims of the invasion. The lost tribe of trust…a small bit of privacy exposed…and taken away. Why? Perhaps for the better good? Is this the Robin Hood of vanity? Perhaps. Perhaps.

> (**BUDDY** *adjust his hair again.*)

To be perfectly honest, I do miss my hair gel, but, if there is someone out there who needs it more than I, who is suffering from some real cosmic hair troubles, I am certainly willing to sacrifice my sense of style for a good cause.

> (*one more hair adjustment*)

Godspeed, Robin.

Scene Ten

(Night.)

*(*JENNY *under the covers.* LOU *beside her.)*

LOU. Wake up, Jenny.
  You were screaming again.

JENNY. I'm sorry.

LOU. You wanna know what you said?

JENNY. No.

LOU. Are you sure?

JENNY. Yes.

LOU. I gotta pee. I keep telling everyone, they need a
  bathroom on this side of the Slabs, but nobody listens.
  I suppose I'd have to build it myself… Which is the kiss
  of death right there. I'll never do it… Or if I started it,
  I wouldn't finish it… That's just how I am… So, I gotta
  trek across fifteen campsites just to relieve myself. My
  life. What a burden.

JENNY. I've yet to see this burden you keep talking about.

LOU. We're sleeping under a tarp.

JENNY. So?

LOU. I got nothing to my name but a suitcase and
  everything that's in it.

JENNY. What's wrong with that?

LOU. I'm forty-five years old.

JENNY. What else do you want?

LOU. House.
  Husband.
  Kids.
  Dogs.
  Garden.
  Money.
  Pursuit of happiness.
  Freedom from want.

Flat screen TV.

George Foreman grill.

JENNY. What do you want all that for?

LOU. Uh, hope.

JENNY. I think you have it pretty good.

LOU. You wanna trade?

JENNY. Maybe.

LOU. You'd trade your kids?

> *(silence)*

You didn't get those saggy boobs from whistling dixie. You nursed some kids.

JENNY. Stop looking at my boobs.

LOU. Don't get paranoid.

> *(silence)*

I just don't understand why you are here. If you have kids to go home to, what the hell are you doing here? Sleeping in this trash heap. Please. Don't you want to go home and see them? Don't you miss them?

JENNY. Of course.

LOU. When's the last time you saw them?

JENNY. Nineteen months.

LOU. Nineteen months? And you're laying here with me, me, of all people, instead of rushing home to see them?

JENNY. Yes.

LOU. Who's been watching them?

JENNY. My mother.

LOU. Where?

JENNY. At my place.

LOU. Where's that?

JENNY. In Oceanside.

LOU. That's just a few hours from here –

JENNY. I know.

LOU. Does she know you're back?

(*silence*)

Listen, I got family troubles myself. I know there are plenty of reasons not to call your mother, and your sister, and four of your brothers, but not calling your kids... Jenny –

JENNY. I don't want to hear it.

LOU. Your kids –

JENNY. I said, I don't want to hear it.

(JENNY *gets out of bed. Looks around for her bag.*)

Where's my stuff?

LOU. I really want you to speak to my shrink Cheryl. Cheryl's done wonders with me. I'm bored to death.

JENNY. It's something I gotta deal with myself.

LOU. It doesn't look like you're dealing with it –

JENNY. You think I should go home and let my kids see this?

LOU. What?

JENNY. *This.*

LOU. Your kids aren't going to care if you have a chicken coming out of your head. They love you.

JENNY. I'm being a better mother by staying away.

LOU. They aren't going to care that you lost your leg, Jenny. They'll be happy to have the rest of you. Don't you think?

JENNY. I hate the rest of me. Where the fuck did you put my stuff?

LOU. I didn't put it anywhere.

JENNY. No one wants to look at me.

(JENNY *has torn the stage apart, finding nothing.*)

(LOU *turns on the light.*)

(JENNY *finds her bag.*)

LOU. I'm looking at you.

JENNY. Men don't. I'm a freak now.

LOU. There's nothing wrong with that.

JENNY. I want my body back.

LOU. You've got what's left of it, Jenny.

> (**LOU** *gets out of bed.*)

JENNY. So what.

LOU. There are plenty of people who love you. And some of them are waiting for you. I'd die for that. Now, if you'll excuse me. My bladder.

> (**LOU** *exits.*)

A burden.

> (**LOU** *exits.*)

> (**JENNY** *drags her stuff beside the bed, and puts her arms around the bag.*)

Scene Eleven

(**LOU** *crawls under a blanket with* **BUDDY**.)

LOU. Put your arms around me, Buddy.

BUDDY. I don't know.

LOU. Please.

BUDDY. But.

LOU. Please.

BUDDY. Lou.

LOU. Buddy.

(**BUDDY** *does it, but it's awkward.*)

Are you comfortable?

BUDDY. No.

LOU. You smell good.

BUDDY. Thank you.

LOU. What kind of soap do you use?

BUDDY. Dial.

LOU. Nice.

(*silence*)

Lot of stars out, huh?

BUDDY. I was just thinking that.

LOU. If I had a quarter for every wish I put on one of those stars…we'd be living in Palm Springs, Buddy… Sleeping under a canopy bed.

BUDDY. I hate Palm Springs.

LOU. That's right. San Diego?

BUDDY. Too crowded.

LOU. Riverside?

BUDDY. Never.

(*silence*)

LOU. I'm not sure how much longer I can sleep with that Jenny. She scares the crap out of me. Shouting and carrying on. I don't know what's going on in her head, but I'm pretty sure it's awful.

BUDDY. I imagine.

LOU. And she tried to kiss Donald.

BUDDY. She must be troubled.

LOU. I know.

BUDDY. Might as well kiss a cement wall.

LOU. Or a turd.

BUDDY. Aluminum siding.

LOU. Or a turd.

BUDDY. She asked me for a kiss too.

> (*silence*)

LOU. Did you give it to her?

BUDDY. No.

> (*silence*)

But I told her to come to me for help. If she wanted.

> (*silence*)

LOU. You are a terrific listener.

> (**BUDDY** *takes his arm back.*)

BUDDY. I don't think she's here for help.

LOU. I don't know what she's here for… But then again, same could be said of me. What am I here for? What's anyone here for?

BUDDY. Free living.

LOU. That.

BUDDY. Good people.

LOU. Yes.

BUDDY. No where else to go.

LOU. Pretty much.

BUDDY. Things could be worse.

LOU. Yes they could.

> (*silence*)

You know, I've met some really great people in my life. I have. I've met some people that I just can't believe they are so nice and wonderful. I really can't. How do they get so nice?

BUDDY. Practice.

LOU. You think?

BUDDY. Yes.

LOU. Maybe… And then there are…there were at least twenty-three people I probably could have really done without meeting.

BUDDY. Uh huh.

LOU. I could have kept on and been better off in life for not having met them. I could be a different person now… But I met them, and I took what came with that. Things they said to me. Things I said to them. Ways they looked at me.

Ways that they touched me, or didn't touch me. How we treated each other. Things I don't like to remember… I think at this point, the things I do want to remember and the things I don't want to remember, are neck and neck in my life, Buddy. They are just about equal in my mind. You think that's the way it is with most people?

BUDDY. I think it's a pretty common battle. Yes.

LOU. I think Jenny is losing the battle.

> *(silence)*

What do you think we should do?

BUDDY. I don't know… Kill her with kindness.

> *(**LOU** moves closer to **BUDDY**, nuzzling in.)*

LOU. Buddy…

> *(**BUDDY** tries to change the subject, know what she's going to ask; begins the hymn, "In The Sweet By and By".)*

BUDDY. *(singing)*
THERE'S A LAND THAT IS FAIRER THAN DAY,
AND BY FAITH WE CAN SEE IT AFAR;

FOR THE FATHER WAITS OVER THE WAY
TO PREPARE US A DWELLING PLACE THERE.

BUDDY & LOU. *(singing)*
"IN THE SWEET BY AND BY,
WE SHALL MEET ON THAT BEAUTIFUL SHORE;
IN THE SWEET BY AND BY,
WE SHALL MEET ON THAT BEAUTIFUL SHORE."

LOU. Do me a favor, Buddy?

BUDDY. Lou. No –

LOU. Kill me with a little kindness.

BUDDY. Lou –

LOU. Take off my clothes.

BUDDY. Now, Lou. No –

LOU. I mean it. I can't live like this any more. It's too hard.

BUDDY. I don't want you to get in trouble.

LOU. I won't.

BUDDY. I don't want you to feel bad about yourself.

LOU. I won't.

BUDDY. I don't want you to go off the deep end somehow.

LOU. I won't.

BUDDY. How do you know?

LOU. I fell off a long time ago.

BUDDY. I don't want you to leave me again.

LOU. I won't. Just take off my clothes and kill me with something interesting.

Scene Twelve

(Morning.)

(JENNY *sits by herself. Ready to use her cell phone.)*

(JENNY *dials.)*

JENNY. Hi Mom… Who'd you think it was? …I'm fine. I'm back… In the States… I just got back… I'm calling you now, aren't I? …Jesus… San Francisco… Uh huh… That's the only flight I could get, so I took it, and I'll just take the bus down… I'm not sure, depends on the bus schedule, and I gotta visit the VA hospital… Well, I have to, they said I have to visit, so…nothing's wrong, it's just part of the procedure, Mom…but I'll call you… well, I don't know, I told you, I don't know what the schedule's like, and how long this VA thing's gonna take, so I can't be sure when I'll get home… I don't want to make any promises… I'm not getting short with you, I'm just trying to tell you the plan, OK? … *(long wait)* How are the girls? – No, no I don't want to talk right now – no, no – please don't put them on, I just don't have time to talk right now but I'll see you guys real soon, OK? I'll be in touch… I love you too, Mom… I will… I'll call.

(She hangs up.)

(JENNY *puts the phone away in her bag. She searches her bag for something else…she finds a camouflage shirt.)*

(The name 'Sutter' is covered in blood.)

Scene Thirteen

(**LOU** *enters with a clipboard, singing the Marine Corps hymn.*)

LOU.

FROM THE HALLS OF MONTEZUMA,
TO THE SHORES OF TRIPOLI,
WE FIGHT OUR COUNTRY'S BATTLES,
IN THE AIR AND LAND AND SEA...

(**BUDDY** *enters with streamers, singing.*)

LOU & BUDDY.

FIRST TO FIGHT FOR RIGHT AND FREEDOM,
AND TO KEEP OUR HONOR CLEAN;
WE ARE PROUD TO CLAIM THE TITLE
OF UNITED STATES MARINE.

(**LOU** *and* **BUDDY** *are ready to stop singing; but* **CHERYL** *enters with balloons, and belts out the end:*)

CHERYL.

HERE'S TO YOU AND TO OUR CORPS,
WHICH WE ARE PROUD TO SERVE;
IN MANY A STRIFE WE'VE FOUGHT FOR LIFE,
AND NEVER LOST OUR NERVE.
IF THE ARMY AND THE NAVY
EVER GAZE ON HEAVEN'S SCENES,
THEY WILL FIND THE STREETS ARE GUARDED
BY UNITED STATES MARINES."

(**LOU** *and* **BUDDY** *stare at her.* **DONALD** *enters.*)

(**LOU** *hands* **DONALD** *a stack of flyers.*)

LOU. OK. What we're going to give her is an old-fashioned hero's welcome.

(**DONALD** *hands back the flyers.*)

DONALD. No can do.

(**BUDDY** *hangs the streamers.*)

(**CHERYL** *begins blowing up balloons.*)

LOU. Donald –

DONALD. I'm a pacifist, man. I don't believe in your hero bullshit.

LOU. This isn't about you.

DONALD. Sorry. I have ideals. I stick to them.

LOU. I thought you were indifferent.

DONALD. Same thing.

LOU. And how far has that gotten you?

DONALD. Blow me. Are you whitening your teeth?

LOU. How many vets you think come through this place?

DONALD. I don't know. I don't care. They sure look whiter, Louise.

LOU. Well, if you ever took the time to talk to people, you might find out that Slab City is a regular stop for quite a few, and it may be high time to give them their due.

DONALD. I thought this was for that Jenny.

LOU. It is, but we're gonna be all inclusive. We're gonna welcome the Vietnam folks home just as well.

DONALD. That's stupid.

LOU. Why?

DONALD. It's too late. Besides, I don't like that Jenny. She's got an edge. I think she's killed people.

LOU. Get out, Donald. Go away.

DONALD. No. I want to watch.

LOU. Why? So you can mock us?

DONALD. Yes.

CHERYL. Mocking is a tell-tale sign of self-esteem issues.

DONALD. Bite me, shrinky dink.

CHERYL. As is name calling.

DONALD. At least my name's not made up.

CHERYL. Pardon?

DONALD. C'mon. Everyone knows your real name's Angie and you're nothing but a washed up hairdresser from

Hemet. The only degree you've got came from Super Cuts.

CHERYL. I help people here.

DONALD. You want to help Lou, give her a perm.

BUDDY. Why don't you move along, Donald.

DONALD. Billy Graham! Save me!

BUDDY. I have a fist. I'll use it.

DONALD. So I hear.

BUDDY. Shut up.

LOU. Donald.

DONALD. This is the best day I've had in a long time.

CHERYL. Now let's all just calm down.

*(***BUDDY*** takes his distance from ***DONALD***.)*

LOU. You are going to send me off the deep end, Donald. I swear. If I hadn't given up fighting, I would kick your ass right now. Smash your face against the –

CHERYL. Lou –

LOU. After I was done smashing your face against the ground, I'd run a bus over your genitals –

CHERYL. The high road is the road paved to peace –

DONALD. Listen to your babysitter, Lou. She's playing doctor.

*(***LOU*** steams.)*

LOU. I am taking the "high road" here, Donald, but let it be known, I don't like you, or the way you act around here.

DONALD. I'll put that in my journal tonight.

LOU. I find you cast a shadow on the entire place.

DONALD. I'll add that as a footnote.

(silence)

*(***LOU*** gathers herself.)*

LOU. Oh, what I'd give for a drink right now.

CHERYL. Lou –

LOU. And I know just where I'd throw it.

CHERYL. The high road.

> (**LOU** *concentrates on her clipboard. Pushes a smile at* **BUDDY**.)

LOU. Buddy, you're in charge of streamers.

BUDDY. I'm on it.

LOU. Cheryl, balloons.

CHERYL. Got it.

LOU. And I think you are also on call for the cake.

CHERYL. Oh, OK –

LOU. I was going to ask Virginia to bake it, but she's out of propane, and Marcus is already bringing beer, and Page can only afford to bring chips, so—

CHERYL. No problem. I'll do it.

LOU. It doesn't have to be anything too fancy, but you know, if you could write something sweet and simple like –

DONALD. "You Risked Your Life For Nothing."

LOU. Like –

DONALD. "I dodged death and all I got was this stupid cake."

LOU. Like –

DONALD. "This Administration doesn't give a rat's ass about you."

LOU. You'll think of something.

CHERYL. Of course.

LOU. (What a burden.)

DONALD. Maybe I'll set up a dunking booth and see if Jenny wants to sit in the dunking seat.

LOU. Buddy, you are in charge of entertainment and the hero's address –

DONALD. Maybe Barry Manilow's available.

LOU. How's that going?

BUDDY. I'll put new batteries in my boombox. Due to a burst of creative expression last night, I'm feeling the inspiration for the address brewing nicely.

LOU. Excellent.

BUDDY. But I may need one more night.

LOU. We don't have one more night.

BUDDY. Maybe just this afternoon.

LOU. That's, that's fine –

DONALD. You guys are screwing again?

(**CHERYL** *loses a balloon mid-blow.*)

LOU. No. Shut up, Donald.

DONALD. I smell a lie.

CHERYL. Lou gave up lying.

LOU. Right. Right. Nothing is happening.

DONALD. Babysitter's mad.

CHERYL. I just wouldn't want you to do anything you'll regret.

LOU. I haven't done anything.

BUDDY. I better go work on the entertainment.

LOU. Thank you, Buddy –

DONALD. Entertainment's right here.

BUDDY. I'd really like to give you a good smack in the jaw, Donald, because if there's anyone in this place who needs it to set him straight, once and for all, it's you –

DONALD. Testify!

BUDDY. But instead, to set a better example of, of, of –

CHERYL. Conflict resolution.

BUDDY. I am taking that goddamn high road.

DONALD. Don't get lost up there. Brother Buddy.

(**BUDDY** *gives him a look that could kill. And exits.*)

LOU. Honest, Cheryl. I'm not lying. Donald's just –

DONALD. Calling a spade, a spade.

(**DONALD** *picks up one of the balloons and blows it up.*)

LOU. Shut up, Donald. Cheryl –

CHERYL. I trust you.

LOU. Good.

CHERYL. I better get started on that cake.

LOU. Thank you, Cheryl.

DONALD. Thank you, Angie.

(*As* **CHERYL** *exits.* **LOU** *is left with* **DONALD.** **JENNY** *enters.*)

JENNY. What's this? –

(**DONALD** *swings like he's playing golf.*)

DONALD. Fore!

(*He pops the balloon.*)

(*Responding to the sound,* **JENNY** *jumps on top of* **LOUISE.**)

(**DONALD** *looks at them, then exits.*)

Scene Fourteen

("Oh Happy Day" by the Edwin Hawkins Singers plays offstage)

(JENNY is curled up in the fetal position. LOU beside her.)

LOU. I really wanted this all to be special for you. That damn Donald. Are you sure you won't join everybody now? Everyone's here.

(silence)

I'm sorry, Jenny. I really did want this to be a special day.

(silence)

This is supposed to be fun.

(BUDDY enters with his boombox, playing the music. He looks at LOU, and begins to exit.)

Damn it. This is going to be fun, Buddy. Please.

(LOU rushes to push him back onstage. Makes him go on. Makes him give his address.)

BUDDY. Uh, Good evening.

(LOU remembers to stop the CD in the boombox. The song stops abruptly. LOU motions for him to continue. BUDDY begins again, not knowing what to say.)

Good evening. Welcome to the official welcome home party for Jenny Sutter.

Uh, Jenny is from the lovely town of Barstow, California, and has just finished a tour of duty in Iraq with the Marine Corps. I, uh, I see a lot of veterans are here tonight, and I just want to say welcome to you too, and thank you for coming. Thank you for being here. We're happy to have you among us... I hope you feel our, our efforts to honor your lives...our efforts...

(BUDDY isn't sure what to say next...)

(silence)

Uh, you know, my uh, my grandfather was a veteran of World War II... There aren't a lot of memories of him. I think I heard him talk all of about ten times. But there is one memory... When I was about six, I picked up a toy rifle and pointed it at him. Just playing, I pointed the rifle at him and said, "Bang, Grandpa. You're dead." And he looked at me with a face I had never seen before... I had never seen his face fall like that, and he said, "I know I am." ...Maybe if I had been old enough, maybe if I'd had the courage, I would have told him, "No you're, not, Grandpa. You're not dead. I see you... I see you breathing... I see your face... I see your hands, and how you can't keep them still... I know you're lonely... I know I'm not much, but... I see you..."

(He stops. Looks directly at **JENNY**.*)*

I see you, Jenny Sutter.

(He looks at the audience; the veterans among us.)

We see you.

(silence)

I know it's not much...this party...this... I'm sorry... It should be more. We should be able to give you so much more than this...

*(***BUDDY*** isn't sure what to say next again. He stares at the audience. He stares at* **LOU**. *Finally,* **LOU** *turns the music on, and "Oh Happy Day" continues to play.)*

(He stares at the audience, as if he wants to say — might find one more thing to say, but just can't figure out what it is.)

*(***CHERYL*** enters with the cake. It's is bright with candles and the words, "JENNY SUTTER.")*

(CHERYL looks around for JENNY. She finally decides to set the cake down.)

(JENNY remains curled up in her corner, LOU beside her.)

(The music continues to play, as BUDDY and CHERYL exit the failed party.)

(LOU leaves JENNY alone.)

(Nothing but JENNY, the cake and the candles, as they slowly burn out with the song.)

(JENNY's cell phone rings; she doesn't answer it.)

Scene Fifteen

(**BUDDY** *finds* **LOU** *alone.*)

BUDDY. Lou.

(**LOU** *eats raisins and lights a cigarette.*)

LOU. Don't get hysterical.

BUDDY. I'm not.

LOU. I just need one.

BUDDY. One is the loneliest number.

LOU. What's that mean?

(**BUDDY** *shrugs.*)

(**LOU** *takes a swig from a flask.*)

Don't blow a gasket. I just need a swig.

BUDDY. Fine.

LOU. Aren't you going to stop me?

BUDDY. No.

LOU. Why not?

BUDDY. I don't want to drink alone.

(**BUDDY** *takes the flask from her.*)

LOU. Whew. Oh boy, that's good.

(**BUDDY** *passes it back.*)

Hell.

(**LOU** *puts out the cigarette.*)

BUDDY. Like old times.

LOU. Some things just can't be fixed.

(*He takes a big swig.*)

BUDDY. A sip for love.

LOU. A sip for luck.

BUDDY. A sip for Jenny.

LOU. Make it a big one.

BUDDY. A sip for my mother. Rest in peace, Mabel.

LOU. You done good, Mabel.

BUDDY. She tried.

(**LOU** *puts her arm around him.*)

LOU. She did.

(*He hands her the flask.*)

You really do need that soap, don't you?

BUDDY. You smell me?

(**BUDDY** *sniffs himself.*)

LOU. Loud and clear.

(*silence*)

BUDDY. Nice lipstick.

LOU. Thank you.

BUDDY. I like that pink.

LOU. I know you do.

BUDDY. You do?

LOU. Why do you think I put it on?

BUDDY. To torture me.

(*silence*)

LOU. Well, that was that, huh?

BUDDY. I guess so.

LOU. Just once I'd like to do something good. Something right. I really would. I'd really like to know what it feels like to actually do something right. Is that so much to ask?

BUDDY. No.

LOU. Give the dog a bone.

BUDDY. You did it right. It just didn't turn out like we had hoped.

LOU. There's an understatement.

BUDDY. It was well-intentioned, Louise.

LOU. Most failures are.

BUDDY. No they're not. Some are poorly designed from the start.

LOU. Maybe.

BUDDY. Besides, ours was a mismatch not a failure.

LOU. What's the difference.
BUDDY. I don't know.

(*silence*)

Balloons.

(**LOU** *nods. They sit in their sense of failure.*)

(**JENNY** *sits up on her side of the stage. She slowly stands. Picks up her duffel bag.*)

(**BUDDY** *puts his arm around her.*)

You do plenty of things right.
LOU. You think so?
BUDDY. I'm crazy about you.

(*She takes a swig of liquor.*)

LOU. Thanks, Stinky.

Scene Sixteen

*(**JENNY**'s cell phone is ringing as she carefully wanders among the balloons and streamers, her heavy bag on her shoulder.)*

(Someone has left a small American flag behind. She picks it up.)

(She sticks the flag in the cake.)

*(**DONALD** enters.)*

DONALD. You figure your shit out?

JENNY. What do you think?

*(**DONALD** tastes a piece of cake. Grabs a balloon.)*

JENNY. Please don't.

DONALD. I'm sorry about that.

(He puts the balloon down, carefully.)

Really man, I'm sorry. I didn't know you'd –

JENNY. Well, neither did I. So there you go.

DONALD. I kinda ruined your party.

(He moves closer to her. Holds out a pair of earrings.)

(She doesn't take them.)

I made them for you. You might as well take them.

(He puts them in her hand.)

(silence)

Aren't you going to put them on?

JENNY. Do I have to?

DONALD. I made them for you.

*(**JENNY** puts on the earrings. They're attractive.)*

That's real turquoise.

(silence)

I found it myself.

(silence)

Out in New Mexico. I like to find my own stones. Makes it more personal.

(silence)

Those are pretty lucky stones. I found them way down in this place no one knows about. Right beside some old petroglyphs. You ever seen a petroglyph?

JENNY. No.

(silence)

DONALD. Indians think turquoise protects people.

JENNY. From what?

DONALD. Harm. Evil spirits. Guys like me.

(silence)

Must be pretty intense.

JENNY. What?

DONALD. *(taps her head)* Whatever that is.

(She moves away.)

(She's about to step on a balloon, but he grabs her.)

I watched my best friend get run over by a ten-wheeler.

JENNY. Can you let go?

DONALD. While I was in buying a cup of coffee. My friend said he'd check the tire pressure in my tires. I was putting a dollar on the counter and looked up, and watched him walk right in front of a truck.

JENNY. So.

DONALD. He was doing me a favor.

JENNY. Let go.

DONALD. It should have been me.

JENNY. Let go.

DONALD. But there was nothing I could do about it.

*(**JENNY** pulls away from him.)*

JENNY. Are you trying to cheer me up?

DONALD. No. Maybe.

JENNY. Jesus.

DONALD. I told you, I don't socialize much.

> (*silence*)

JENNY. I'm sorry about your friend, but I'm not really interested –

DONALD. Sometimes god-awful horrible things happen and there is no good reason for it, and there isn't dog shit you can do to change it. Nothing. You just gotta…you just gotta…you just gotta…suck it up, forget about it –

JENNY. I killed fifteen people because I didn't check a baby's diaper. A woman let her baby be the bomb. Suck that up. A kid's head got blown off. Teeth and brains everywhere. My friends. Forget that.

> (*silence*)

DONALD. You do have a point.

JENNY. So if you don't mind, please skip the "pick me ups".

DONALD. Still, there's nothing you can do about it now. It's done. That's reality. Where you face what you can and cannot do. What you can and cannot change. Reality. The real world.

JENNY. And is that what you're doing, out here in this desert freak show? Facing reality? The real world?

DONALD. No, I'm avoiding it. At all costs.

JENNY. Then you don't know what the hell you're talking about.

DONALD. No.

JENNY. Jesus.

DONALD. I just hear that's the way it's done.

JENNY. Thanks.

DONALD. You're welcome.

JENNY. Have you seen Lou?

DONALD. No.

JENNY. Do you know how I might go about finding her –

DONALD. Louise!

JENNY. That's one way –

DONALD. LOUISE! STOP HAVING SEX WITH BUDDY! JENNY SUTTER IS LOOKING FOR YOU! SHE'S LEAVING!

JENNY. Who said I was leaving?

DONALD. That's the easiest way to find someone around here.

JENNY. Who said I was leaving?

DONALD. I did.

JENNY. What if I want to stay?

DONALD. I'm telling you to go.

JENNY. So?

> *(silence)*

What if I don't want to go yet?

DONALD. You can't keep that phone away.

JENNY. I could turn it off.

DONALD. You won't. No one turns them off.

JENNY. The battery could die.

DONALD. They'd still call. You'd still hear it. Hell, I come all the way out here, for some peace and quiet, and I still hear a fucking cell phone. Shit.

JENNY. I have kids.

DONALD. Oh, everyone's got some fucking reason. "I'm a doctor. It's my job." "My father's sick." "My boyfriend said he was going to call." … "I'm important."

> **(JENNY** *smiles.)*

Heaven forbid missing a goddamn phone call. World could end.

> *(silence)*

Those earrings look good on you. I did a nice job on those.

JENNY. Thank you.

DONALD. You're pretty.

> *(silence)*

You still want that kiss?

JENNY. Not really.

DONALD. The sun is down.

JENNY. So.

DONALD. You're leaving.

JENNY. I really don't want to kiss you.

DONALD. I think it's only appropriate.

> *(silence)*

I owe it to you.

JENNY. I got the earrings. And your plum advice. I think you've given me more than I can handle, Donald.

DONALD. Would a kiss hurt?

JENNY. From you? Seems like it could.

DONALD. It could be just what you're looking for.

JENNY. Could kill me.

DONALD. It could be what you came out here to find.

JENNY. You think so?

DONALD. No. But we can pretend.

JENNY. You have no idea what you're talking about, do you?

DONALD. None. No.

JENNY. You just say things, willy-nilly.

DONALD. Most of the time. Yes.

JENNY. That's stupid.

DONALD. It fills the gap.

JENNY. What gap?

DONALD. Where I used to be.

> *(**DONALD** moves closer.)*

I'm not good with people anymore.

> *(He kisses her. It's wonderful.)*

But I miss them.

> *(He kisses her again.)*

I miss them a lot.

> *(She kisses him.)*

Welcome home.

> *(He leaves her alone.)*

(She picks up her bag, and looks around to exit, when she stops and tries to scratch her prosthetic leg.)

*(**BUDDY** enters with a broom.)*

BUDDY. I hear you're leaving.

JENNY. Well.

*(**BUDDY** points to her leg.)*

BUDDY. You're the bionic woman.

JENNY. I told them, don't give me that metal shit. I want something that looks real.

BUDDY. It looks real.

JENNY. It looks like what it is.

*(**JENNY** covers her leg.)*

What are my kids going to think?

BUDDY. They'll want to try it on.

JENNY. No.

BUDDY. I'm serious. Kids love that stuff.

(silence)

Lou's packing up. She wants to go with you. See you get home alright.

JENNY. Why?

BUDDY. Says it's time for a trip.

JENNY. She just got here.

BUDDY. Well, that's Lou. She giveth, and she taketh away.

(silence)

Cheryl's gonna give you two a ride to the station. All the way to L.A.

JENNY. She doesn't have to do that.

BUDDY. Sometimes a long drive out of here is welcome.

(silence)

I just wanted to say it was a real pleasure to meet you, Jenny. Thanks for coming out to Slab City. I wish you the best. I really do.

JENNY. Thanks, Buddy.

BUDDY. Come back any time.

> *(silence)*

JENNY. I enjoyed your sermons.

BUDDY. I see people sleeping.

JENNY. Probably just hung over.

BUDDY. I don't know why I feel the need to ramble on about things all the time… Afraid… Maybe if I don't…

> *(silence)*

That blue or red will swallow me up.

> *(silence)*

JENNY. You're a good preacher.

BUDDY. Well. It only cost $9.99.

> *(silence)*

> *(**JENNY**'s cell phone rings again. She ignores it. **BUDDY** waits for it to stop.)*

You're gonna be OK, Jenny Sutter. I promise you. I'm telling you. You will be OK.

> *(**JENNY** takes them both off-guard when she hugs him.)*

JENNY. I appreciate you and Lou…being so… I really… I don't really know what I'm doing right now… Or who I am… My head is – my body is – I'm afraid all the time – I basically just want to lay down and cry. But I can't really do that. I need to get home. I have responsibilities. My kids.

> *(**JENNY** exits.)*

> *(**BUDDY** sweeps the stage, sings hymn, "Come All Ye Tender-Hearted".)*

BUDDY. *(singing)*
COME ALL YOU TENDER-HEARTED
YOUR ATTENTION I WILL CALL
I'LL TELL YOU HOW IT STARTED
COME LISTEN ONE AND ALL.

*(***CHERYL** *enters and joins the song, and the cleaning of the stage.)*

BUDDY & CHERYL.

LAST WEDNESDAY NIGHT, THERE WAS A LIGHT
SEEN SHINING ON A HILL
A MOTHER RAN WITH ALL HER MIGHT
WHILE EVERYTHING WAS STILL.

*(***DONALD** *enters and joins the song, and the cleaning of the stage.)*

BUDDY, CHERYL & DONALD.

SHE WENT INTO A NEIGHBOR'S HOUSE
SOME HUNDRED YARDS AWAY
SHE SAT DOWN AND TALKED WITH THEM
BUT SHE DID NOT MEAN TO STAY.

*(***LOU** *enters and joins the song.)*

BUDDY, CHERYL, DONALD & LOU.

DON'T STAY TOO LONG DEAR MOTHER THERE
FOR WE'LL BE LONESOME HERE
"I'LL GET SOME LINIMENT," SHE SAID.
"THEN I'LL RETURN AGAIN,"
BUT WHEN SHE STARTED HOME AGAIN
HER HOUSE WAS IN A FLAMES
SHE CRIED, "OH LORD MY BABIES ARE GONE
AND I'M THE ONE TO BLAME."

*(***LOU** *exits.)*

BUDDY, CHERYL & DONALD.

SHE BURST IN ALL ASUNDER THEN
AND THE FLAMES ROLLED O'ER HER HEAD
SHE CRIED, "OH LORD HOW SAD THEY SLEEP
WRAPPED UP IN A RED HOT FLAME."

BUDDY, CHERYL, DONALD & HUGO. *(offstage)*

THEIR LITTLE BONES LAY ON THE GROUND
THEY BOTH LAY FACE TO FACE…

Scene Seventeen

HUGO. *(singing)*
"EACH OTHER DID ENTWINE
EACH OTHER DID EMBRACE"

> *(The bus station.)*

> *(**HUGO** is asleep.)*

> *(**JENNY** enters, followed by **LOU** dragging her suitcase on stage.)*

LOU. Did you see that?

JENNY. What?

LOU. Cheryl giving me the silent treatment. The whole time. There is nothing I hate worse than the silent treatment. Hit me with a two-by-four, but don't hit me with that tight lip and blank stare. That ice can really send me over the edge.

JENNY. You really don't need to do this.

LOU. Things were getting little hot in the Slab kitchen anyway.

> *(**LOU** digs through her suitcase and unloads all the stolen toiletries mentioned in **BUDDY**'s speech, and lays them at **JENNY**'s feet, one by one.)*

Page. Ricky. Raoul. Marcus. Linda. Pete. Tony. Virginia. Some guy in the third ten. I don't know who.

> *(until she finally finds the shoelace)*

Jenny.

> *(**LOU** hands it to **JENNY**.)*

Sorry.

JENNY. You can have it.

LOU. When you deny yourself everything you really want, you start wanting the craziest shit. I swear. Want just replaces want with some other kind of want. When you keep yourself away from people, you start wanting to take their most intimate things. To get closer. And so you start trying to get that, whatever it is. Just for the hell of it. Just to see if you can get it. To see if people will miss it. Turns out, they do. I heard more people complain about missing their tweezers. And soap. Soap seems to be pretty essential.

> (**LOU** *pulls a final bar of Dial soap from the stolen toiletries, and smells it.*)

I love that Buddy.

> (**LOU** *pulls the deck of playing cards from her bag and hands them to* **JENNY**.)

Shuffle those cards, Jenny Sutter, I'm going to show you how it's done.

JENNY. You think so, huh?

> (**JENNY** *shuffles the cards and hands them back to* **LOU**. **LOU** *deals.*)

LOU. I've played Gin from Eureka to Baja.

> (*They study their cards.*)

JENNY. You should have stayed.

LOU. Don't be silly.

> (**JENNY** *cell phone rings. She doesn't answer it. They wait for it to stop.*)

JENNY. I think I should go the rest of the way home alone, Lou.

> (*silence*)

LOU. That's fine.

JENNY. I'm sorry, but it's a small apartment. We haven't been together… And I don't know what's…

LOU. Please, I understand. I've got plenty of places to go. Places I haven't been yet. I could check out Big Sur. I've never been there.

JENNY. I hear it's beautiful.

LOU. Yeah, me too.

> *(silence)*

Cliffs. Waves. Hippies. Nothing wrong with that.

> *(***LOU*** *lays down her cards.*)

Gin.

JENNY. Motherfucker.

LOU. Gin. See? Now, don't let me play another hand.

JENNY. I won't.

LOU. I mean it.

> *(***JENNY*** *takes the cards.*)

JENNY. I appreciate what you've done for me. You're a good person –

> *(***LOU*** *taps her suitcase.*)

LOU. Look at me. A petty thief. Fallen off the wagon. But, my eyebrows look pretty good. Nice and plucked. And my teeth. White, huh? –

JENNY. Giving me a place to stay. Putting up with me. My nightmares.

> *(***LOU*** *kneels down and puts the shoelace back in* ***JENNY****'s shoe.*)

LOU. OK. Those I won't miss. You said some crazy things. You wanna know what you said?

JENNY. Not really –

LOU. "Give me something to believe in."

> *(silence)*

"Give me something to believe in." Three of four times one night. Five, six times another night.

JENNY. Really.

LOU. The strange thing is, I feel that way all the time, Jenny. All the time. I hear those exact same words in my head all the time. Like a chant, constantly, "Give me something to believe in. Give me something to believe in. Give me something to believe in." I wanted to wake you up, but I thought you might tell me who you were talking to.

JENNY. Did I?

LOU. No. You left me hanging… Maybe it's that same stranger I'm looking for…chanting to… Anything who might answer. Anyone who's listening. Anyone. Someone. Wanderers. Angels. Birds. Dogs. Babies. Buddy.

JENNY. What do you do with it?

LOU. Just keep chanting it, I guess.

(**LOU** *ties the shoelace.*)

Something's going to come of it. Someday. We'll believe in something big and wonderful. Something really terrific is going to come along.

(**LOU** *touches* **JENNY***'s prosthetic leg.*)

Something bigger than all this.

(*The sound of the bus offstage.*)

(**HUGO** *wakes, abruptly.*)

HUGO. Oceanside! Who's going to Oceanside! Hurry up!

(*He stomps a bug as he exits.*)

JENNY. That's me.

LOU. Looks like it.

JENNY. Well.

LOU. You take care of yourself.

(**JENNY** *picks up her stuff.*)

I'll be thinking of you.

JENNY. Thanks for everything, Lou. I love you.

LOU. Don't try and make me cry. (What a burden.)

(**LOU** *watches* **JENNY** *exit.*)

(*singing*)

WE SHALL SING ON THAT BEAUTIFUL SHORE
THE MELODIOUS SONGS OF THE BLESSED;
AND OUR SPIRITS SHALL SORROW NO MORE,
NOT A SIGH FOR THE BLESSING OF REST.

IN THE SWEET BY AND BY,
WE SHALL MEET ON THAT BEAUTIFUL SHORE;
IN THE SWEET BY AND BY,
WE SHALL MEET ON THAT BEAUTIFUL SHORE.

(blackout)

End of Play

AFTERWORD

I began writing *Welcome Home, Jenny Sutter* in 2006, with the several questions in mind; questions that I still have, that have not been answered as we premiere this play in February of 2008. As a nation at war, how are we treating our returning veterans? Are we ready for the first generation of women veterans wounded and maimed by combat? What is our responsibility, as citizens, to those who are serving in this war; a war that many feel was a mistake from the start, that has been costly, poorly planned, a waste of both our human and financial resources, and, which has no end in sight? What are we to DO about it, as individuals, as citizens, that goes beyond politics, that might give some sort of comfort or aid or understanding to those who have suffered and sacrificed themselves for this war? I feel that this play is a portrait and a song of these questions. It is a story of a few people trying to figure out, in their way, how to make one woman's return home more humane and welcome and loving, so that she can begin to return to herself, and to her children. It is my humble attempt, as a playwright, to give a voice to warrior where I feel silence has become the accepted means of communication between our nation and our warriors. I fear that silence is strangling us. We need to find new ways to talk about war so there remains no doubt as to just how devastating it is to our people and our culture. And maybe, just maybe, the powers that be will be less cavalier about starting the next conflict. Maybe. Or maybe they will end this war before the next Jenny Sutter is called back to the desert, and this cycle of broken spirits continues. I am trying to remain hopeful.

Julie Marie Myatt
Ashland, OR
February 18, 2008